Jack Frost's
Ice Castle
Ocean World
Sealife Centre
Seals
Dolphins
Baby
Turtles
Leamouth Pier
Penguins
Ice floes
South Pole

The Magical Conch Shell at my side,
I'll rule the oceans far and wide!
But my foolish goblins have shattered the shell,
So now I cast my icy spell.

Seven shell fragments, be gone, I say,
To the human world to hide away,
Now the shell is gone, it's plain to see,
The oceans will never have harmony!

Ally the Dolphin Fairy

by Daisy Meadows

The Fairyland Palace
GALA
FAIRYLAND ROYAL AQUARIUM
Fairyland Royal Aquarium
Kirsty's Gran's House
Lighthouse
The Park
Rockpool
Ocean Star Sailing Ship
Lea-On-Sea
Whales

Contents

Off to Fairyland

Kirsty Tate and Rachel Walker stepped off the bus and blinked in the sunshine. The two girls were staying with Kirsty's gran in Leamouth for the spring holiday and today they'd come to Lea-on-Sea, a small seaside resort along the coast. "I've got some shopping to do, so I'll meet you back here at midday," Kirsty's gran said, getting off the bus. "Have fun!"

"We will," Kirsty assured her. "See you later, Gran." Then she turned to Rachel. "Come on, let's go down to the beach!"

It took the girls just moments to walk down the sandy steps to the curving bay, which was packed with families enjoying the sun. The sky was a clear, fresh blue, and a breeze ruffled the tops of the waves. Lots of children were swimming in the sea, while shrieking seagulls soared above them, their strong white wings stretched wide.

"It's lovely," Rachel said, slipping off her shoes and wiggling her bare toes in the warm sand. She pointed to the far edge of the bay. "Let's go over there, shall we? It's a bit less crowded."

The girls made their way across the beach, zigzagging between deckchairs, windbreaks and sandcastles. Then Kirsty stopped walking suddenly and bent down. "Hey, look at this shell," she said, picking it up to show Rachel. "It's really sparkly."

Rachel peered at the fan-shaped scallop shell, which was a creamy-white colour with pink edging. And yes – tiny golden sparkles were fizzling all over it!

Rachel's heart quickened with excitement as she looked at Kirsty. "That looks like fairy magic," she whispered.

"Just what I was thinking," Kirsty replied, smiling. "Oh! And I can feel something underneath it, too."

She flipped the shell over in her palm and both girls saw a tiny golden scroll tucked into it, tied with a pretty red ribbon. Rachel untied the ribbon and unfurled the scroll, then both girls leaned over to read the tiny writing there.

"*King Oberon and Queen Titania hereby invite you to the Fairyland Ocean Gala,*" Kirsty read in a whisper. "Oh, wow!"

Rachel felt a rush of excitement. She and Kirsty had been to Fairyland many times now, and had enjoyed lots of wonderful fairy adventures, but the thought of visiting their fairy friends was always a treat. "What are we waiting for?" she said. "Let's hide behind these rocks so nobody sees us – and go to Fairyland!"

Once they were hidden from view, Rachel and Kirsty opened the pretty golden lockets they wore. The lockets had been a present from the fairy king and queen and contained magical fairy dust, which would transport the girls to Fairyland. Their fingers trembling with excitement, the two friends each took a pinch of the sparkling pink dust and sprinkled themselves with it.

Instantly, a glittering whirlwind spun up about them, and they felt themselves shrink smaller and smaller to fairy-size. Kirsty just managed to grab Rachel's hand, as they whizzed around very quickly. Then, after a few moments, the whirlwind dropped and the girls felt themselves lowered gently to the ground.

"Another beach!" Rachel exclaimed in delight, gazing around. "A Fairyland beach!"

"And we're fairies!" Kirsty cried, fluttering the beautiful gauzy wings on her back, loving the way that they shimmered all the colours of the rainbow in the sunlight. The two friends were standing on the beach next to the Fairyland Royal Aquarium, an unusual building made of glass and stone, and the Gala was in full swing. Hundreds of fairies were dancing to lively music, competing in fun swimming races, enjoying boat rides, and tucking in to the most wonderful-looking ice creams.

"There are the Party Fairies," Kirsty said, spotting their old friends flitting about, making sure that everyone was having fun. "Oh, and there's Shannon the Ocean Fairy!"

Rachel and Kirsty had met Shannon during a very special summer adventure, which had taken place last time they'd holidayed in Leamouth. Shannon was fluttering towards them now, followed by some other fairies the girls didn't recognise. "Hello Kirsty, hello Rachel!" Shannon cried happily. "It's lovely to see you again. These fairies are my Ocean Fairy helpers, who take care of the creatures in the Royal Aquarium – and throughout all the oceans, too!"

Shannon introduced the fairies – Ally the Dolphin Fairy, Amelie the Seal Fairy, Pia the Penguin Fairy, Tess the Sea Turtle Fairy, Stephanie the Starfish Fairy, Whitney the Whale Fairy and Courtney the Clownfish Fairy.

"Hi," said Whitney, who was wearing a

brightly patterned dress. "Have you been to one of our ocean parties before?"

"No," Kirsty replied. "But this one looks great! Are you celebrating something special?"

"We hold a Gala like this every summer," explained Tess, who had long blonde hair in two plaits. "It's lots of fun, but important too. Shannon plays a tune on the Golden Conch Shell which ensures peace and harmony throughout the ocean for the whole year. It's up there, look."

Tess was pointing at a small stage in front of the Aquarium, with a table in the middle, covered in a midnight-blue velvet cloth. On top of the cloth sat a large golden shell, which glittered with magic.

"Talking of which...it's about time I began," said Shannon. She winked at Rachel and Kirsty. "Wish me luck!"

As Shannon walked onstage, a hush fell over the party. "Good afternoon, everyone," Shannon said in her tinkling voice. "I hope you're all having a lovely time at our annual Ocean Gala."

"No!" came a bad-tempered voice just then. "No, I am not having a good time, actually!"

Rachel's mouth fell open in shock as a grumpy-looking figure barged through the crowd and onto the stage. "Jack Frost!" she hissed. "What's he doing here?"

Kirsty bit her lip. Horrid Jack Frost was such a trouble-maker! "I don't know," she replied in a whisper, "but it looks like we're about to find out."

Shattered!

"Excuse me..." Shannon said politely, but Jack Frost grabbed the microphone and began addressing the crowd.

"I hate the ocean!" he ranted. "I can't swim, and I detest getting sand between my toes. It's no fun for me, so I don't see why I should let you lot enjoy yourselves. Lads – to work!" he ordered.

At his words, a group of five goblins

rushed onstage and grabbed the Golden Conch Shell, hurrying away with it before Shannon or any of the other Ocean Fairies could stop them. But in true goblin style, they immediately began arguing about which way to go, and who was going to carry it. The goblins pulled the shell back and forth between them until, as a result of their struggles, it suddenly flew high into the air...and smashed to the ground, breaking into pieces.

Shannon ran over to collect the pieces of the broken shell but Jack Frost was too fast for her.

"The shell may be shattered, but I don't care. I'll scatter its pieces everywhere!" he chanted, waving his wand at the fragments of shell. A blast of icy magic burst from his wand, spiralling and whirling around the seven broken pieces and sending them flying into the air. Then, they were gone.

"Your precious shell is scattered all over the human world now," Jack Frost sneered.

"You'll never find the pieces and your ocean world will be forever in chaos!" Then, with another wave of his wand and a horrible cackle of laughter, he and his goblins vanished from sight.

Shannon had turned very pale. "This is awful," she said anxiously. "Until I can play the Golden Conch Shell, the ocean will be in a terrible state! All the creatures will be confused – they won't be able to find their homes or families... What are we going to do?"

Queen Titania stepped onto the stage and put a comforting arm around Shannon. "Don't worry," she said. "I can't stop Jack Frost's spell, but I'll do my best to alter it. Come, let us go to the Royal Aquarium, and I'll explain my plan. Ocean Fairies, you come too," she said. Then her eyes fell upon Kirsty and Rachel and her serious expression softened. "Hello, my dears," she added. "Would you join us, as well? We need your help again."

Kirsty and Rachel both bobbed curtseys. "Of course," Kirsty said politely.

They followed the queen into the huge entrance hall of the Royal Aquarium, which had a polished marble floor, and lots of glass tanks arranged along one side. The windows at the top of the hall were of stained glass, and featured pictures of different sea creatures – mighty whales, leaping dolphins, dainty seahorses, and many more. Sunlight streamed through

them, casting colourful reflections onto the floor.

The glass tanks varied in size, and each housed a single creature: a dolphin, a seal, a penguin, a starfish, a turtle, a whale and a clownfish. All seven creatures were surrounded by faint golden sparkles, Kirsty noticed.

"This is my plan," Queen Titania announced. "These are the seven Magical Ocean Creatures who are the companions of our Ocean Fairies. I now proclaim them the guardians of the seven pieces of the Golden Conch Shell." She waved her wand and a jet of silver magic burst from its tip and swirled around the Aquarium.

The light from the magic was so bright, Rachel had to shut her eyes – and when she opened them again, the tanks were empty. The Magical Ocean Creatures had gone!

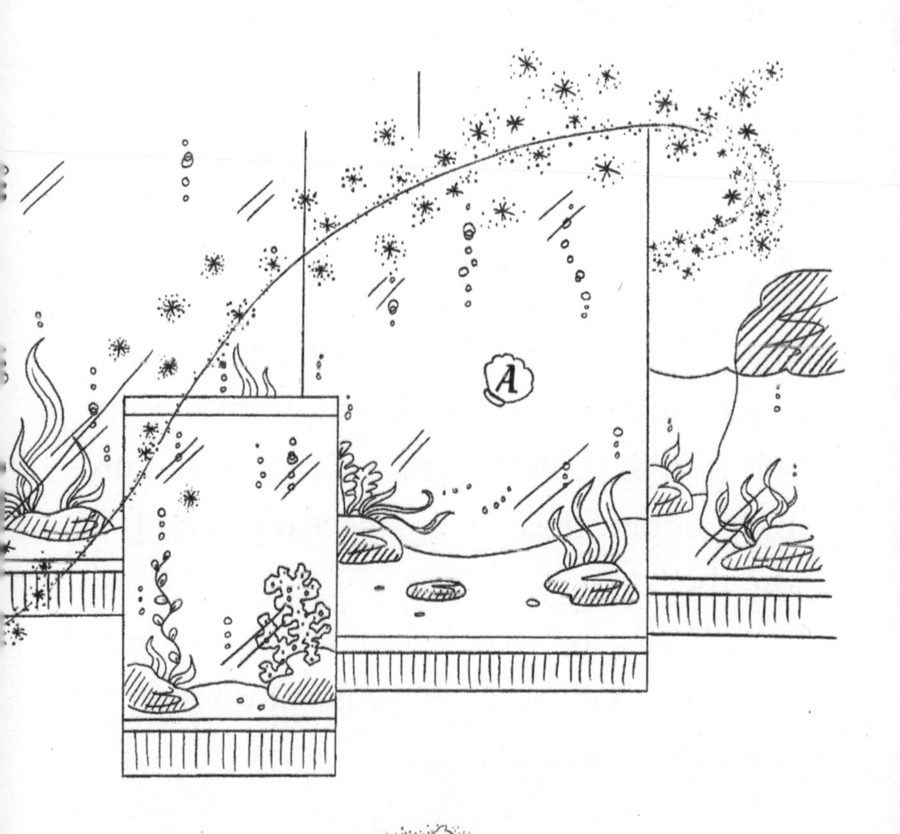

"Where are they all?" dark-haired Ally gasped, peering at the tank where her dolphin had been swimming just moments earlier. "Where's Echo?"

"I have sent all seven creatures out into the human world," the queen said. "They will become the right size for the world, and will find themselves near a piece of the Golden Conch Shell. My fairies, your job is to find the Magical Ocean Creatures once again, and each collect a piece of the shell."

"We'll help," Rachel said, feeling a rush of excitement at the thought of another fairy adventure.

"Thank you," the queen said, smiling at Rachel and Kirsty. Then she turned to Ally. "I will send you out first," she declared. "Kirsty and Rachel will help you look for Echo. Good luck!"

She pointed her wand at Ally, then at the two girls, and a glittering whirlwind immediately lifted them off their feet and spun them up into the air.

Where's Echo?

When Kirsty and Rachel landed, they were back to their usual sizes, and were standing outside a building called 'Ocean World'. "It's a sea-life centre," Kirsty realised, reading a nearby poster. "This says 'See the ocean creatures, with our amazing underwater tunnels and the unique ocean-side stadium'. Perfect!"

"Echo must be inside somewhere," Ally said from where she was fluttering near Rachel's shoulder. She looked rather like a glittering butterfly, with her beautiful long silver dress and sparkly wings, Kirsty thought. "Come on, let's go in."

Kirsty's gran had given the girls some spending money and luckily they had just enough to pay the entrance fee, so in they went, with Ally tucking herself into Rachel's pocket so that she'd be out of sight. As they walked through the Aquarium, they couldn't help noticing that the ocean creatures were acting very strangely. "Look," Rachel said in surprise, stopping in front of one glass tank filled with tropical fish.

"These angel fish are turning somersaults!"

Kirsty stared. Sure enough, the pretty striped fish were swimming loop-the-loops in the water – and looked very dizzy!

Then, further along, they saw three catfish in a tank who were tickling each other with their whiskers, and some octopuses whose tentacles were all tangled together in knots.

"This is awful," Ally said, looking worried. "And it's all because Shannon didn't get to play her tune on the Golden Conch Shell. We've got to find the pieces to put the conch together again as soon as possible."

Just then, an announcement came over the tannoy system. "Ladies and gentlemen, our wonderful Wild Dolphin Show is about to begin – please take your seats in the ocean-side stadium!"

"Dolphins?" Kirsty said excitedly. "Echo might be there. Come on!"

The girls and Ally quickly made their way to the ocean-side stadium. It was an open-air arena with a wonderful view down to the sea. A wooden jetty had been built close to the water, and the girls saw some boys in Ocean World uniforms there, carrying buckets of fish.

A couple of dolphin trainers strode on to the jetty and waved at the audience. "Hi, everyone!" one of them called. She had a blonde ponytail and a big smile. "Welcome to the Ocean World Wild Dolphin Show, where you're going to see dolphins performing some amazing tricks."

"These dolphins are wild dolphins, who live freely in the ocean," said the second trainer, a man with short brown hair. "But they love showing what they can do – and they love their dinner too!" He grinned and threw a handful of fish into the sea, and immediately a group of dolphins appeared, swimming gracefully in and out of the water.

"I love the way they look like they're smiling," Rachel said, her eyes glued to the beautiful creatures.

"Me too," Ally said, peeping out of her hiding place in Rachel's pocket.

"But I can't see Echo anywhere," she added, sounding disappointed.

"For our first trick, the dolphins are going to jump through this hoop," the first trainer announced, showing the audience a bright red hoop. "They love doing this – just watch!" She held the hoop out above the water expectantly... But the dolphins didn't seem interested. In fact, they completely ignored the trainer and her hoop.

The trainer looked a bit embarrassed. "Hey, guys," she coaxed the dolphins, waving the hoop around. "Over here!"

Ally shook her head. "Oh dear," she whispered. "This is because the Golden Conch Shell is missing, I know it. The dolphins look really confused."

It soon became clear that the dolphins didn't want to jump through the hoop, or balance beach balls on their noses, or do any tricks at all. "I'm really sorry, everybody," the man with brown hair said, "but we'll have to cancel today's show. I don't know what's wrong with the dolphins – they usually love performing!"

A sigh of disappointment went up from the audience, and people got to their feet to leave. Rachel stood up too, but Kirsty grabbed her hand to stop her. "Wait," she said. "Look at those boys."

Rachel and Ally peered down to see what Kirsty had noticed. The two boys who'd been carrying the buckets of fish were messing about on the jetty now, throwing fish at each other. One boy's cap fell off, and the girls and Ally gasped as they saw what a pointy nose the boy had...and what green skin, too!

"They're goblins!" Rachel realised, her stomach lurching at the sight. What were they doing there?

"Oh no," Ally cried. "Jack Frost must have realised that Queen Titania changed the spell. He's sent his goblins into the human world to get the missing shell pieces before we do!"

Goblins Underwater

The three friends fell silent. This was terrible news! They couldn't let the goblins find the missing shell pieces first. But then Ally spoke again, and this time she sounded much more cheerful. "Oh look, there's Echo! Do you see that sweet little dolphin following the others?"

Rachel and Kirsty peered down at the sea. The group of dolphins were heading away from the stadium, and behind them swam a small, pretty dolphin, whose silvery coat sparkled in the sunshine. "The piece of shell must be somewhere nearby," Kirsty realised. "We've got to get in the water and go after her."

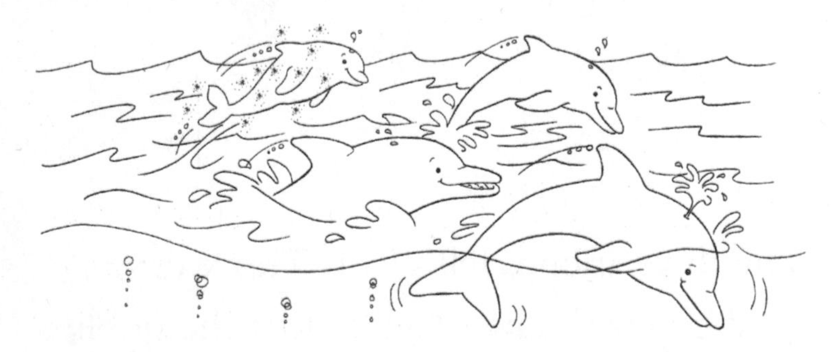

Ally smiled and a dimple flashed in her cheek. "No sooner said than done," she declared. She waved her wand and silver sparkly fairy dust flowed around Kirsty and Rachel...turning them into fairies again! "Now you need one of these each," she said, waving her wand again and conjuring up two magic bubbles. The bubbles settled over the girls' heads, like diving helmets, then disappeared with a pop. Rachel and Kirsty knew from their adventures with Shannon that they would now be able to breathe underwater, and that they would stay warm and dry!

"Ready? Let's go!" said Ally. Then the three of them flew to the sea and plunged into the water after Echo and the other dolphins. Rachel grinned at Kirsty as they swam through the cool clear water.

What an adventure this was turning out to be!

The three fairies followed the dolphins deep into the ocean, all the way to a beautiful underwater grotto, full of colourful sea anemones and waving fronds of seaweed. Ally gave a high whistle, and Echo turned her head.

At the sight of her fairy mistress there in the grotto, Echo made a happy clicking sound and swam over at once, looking delighted to see her. Ally gave Echo a hug and stroked her silvery nose. "Hello there," she said, smiling. "Have you seen the piece of Golden Conch Shell anywhere?"

Echo shook her head. "I've asked the other dolphins, but they just seem really confused by everything," she replied. "I haven't searched this grotto yet though. Maybe we can do that together."

The friends swam further into the cave and began looking all over it in search of a piece of the Golden Conch Shell.

"There's something glittering down there," Kirsty said excitedly, pointing at one corner of the cave floor. "I wonder if it might be the shell?"

But just as they were about to go and take a closer look, Ally hissed a warning. "There are divers heading this way," she said. "Hide!"

She, Kirsty and Rachel immediately darted behind a large clump of seaweed so that the divers wouldn't see them. The girls knew that the existence of the fairies had to be kept a closely guarded secret from other humans.

The two divers swam closer. The light was dim down in the ocean but Rachel couldn't help noticing what big feet they had – so big, in fact, that they had no need for flippers. Then she realised that the divers' skin looked rather green-ish, too...

She elbowed Kirsty. "They're goblins!" she whispered. "And I think they've seen the shell!"

A Sparkling Shell

Rachel was right. The divers were goblins – and they were heading straight for the sparkling piece of shell that lay in the corner of the cave. "Quick!" Kirsty cried. "We've got to get there first!"

The three fairies and Echo swam as fast as they could towards the shimmering piece of shell – but before they or the goblins could reach it, a small pink crab scuttled over and picked up the shell piece in its pincers.

"That's definitely part of the Golden Conch," Ally said in excitement, as sparkles of light streaked through the water from the shell. "Come on!"

Before the fairies could get there, though, the goblins reached the crab, and one of them held out his hand. "Give it here, Stalk-Eyes," he ordered rudely.

The little crab held tight to the shell, and some other, bigger crabs emerged from behind a rock and formed a protective circle around their friend, snapping with their pincers to keep the goblins away.

"How can we get rid of those goblins?" Rachel wondered, as one of them made a grab for the piece of shell. She turned to Ally. "Could Echo and the other dolphins chase them away, do you think?"

Ally smiled. "You bet," she said, and whispered something to Echo. Echo nodded, her mouth falling open in a smile, and she made a series of clicks and whistling sounds to the other dolphins.

Immediately all the dolphins rushed towards the goblins, who looked absolutely terrified at the sight. "Don't eat me!" cried one. "Help! Swim for your life!"

"Aaaarrrghh!" screamed the other goblin. "Mummy!"

Thc frightened goblins turned and swam off as fast as they could, and Rachel grinned. She loved it when a plan worked out!

"Now we just need to persuade the little crab to play swapsies," Ally said thoughtfully, picking up a small stone from the seabed. She waved her wand and a stream of silvery lights danced through the water from the wand, and all around the stone...turning it into a gleaming white pearl!

Ally swam over to the crab. "Look at this beautiful pearl," she said, holding it out to show him. "Would you like to swap it for that piece of broken shell?"

The crab dropped the piece of Golden Conch Shell at once and picked up the pearl, looking very excited.

"Thank you," Kirsty smiled, reaching out to take the piece of shell.

"Look out!" Rachel shouted suddenly, as the goblins, followed by Echo and the other dolphins, careered back into the grotto. The goblins and dolphins were going so fast that they caused a current of

water to surge through the cave – which lifted the piece of shell right off the seabed and sent it whizzing away from the three fairies.

Kirsty made a lunge, but before she could grab the piece of shell, a goblin snatched it up and swam quickly out of the grotto.

"After him!" called Ally. "Don't let him get away!"

Kirsty, Rachel, Ally and Echo immediately gave chase. The goblin swam all the way up to the surface and, as the others followed, they suddenly heard a lot of noise. Once their heads broke the surface of the water, they realised why.

"It's a water-skiing display!" Kirsty cried in alarm, swerving to avoid a speedboat that roared past her. All around them were speedboats whizzing along, towing water-skiers behind them, and up on the beach, a crowd of spectators were watching the action.

Just then, the girls saw one water-skier zoom right past the goblin who was holding the piece of Golden Conch Shell. He stretched out a hand and grabbed the piece of conch as he whizzed by…and they realised that he was a goblin too.

They watched in dismay as he zoomed away at a tremendous speed. "We're never going to catch up with him," Rachel said. "There's no way we can swim that fast."

"No," said Ally, "but the dolphins can, can't they?" She grinned and leapt out of the water and onto Echo's back, taking hold of the strong fin. Then she gave a whistle and two other dolphins swam over to Kirsty and Rachel. "Ladies – your carriages await," Ally smiled. "Jump on board!"

Kirsty and Rachel didn't need telling twice! They both fluttered out of the water and onto their own dolphins, clinging tight to their fins. "And off we go," Ally cheered. "Come on, Echo!"

Echo and the two other dolphins surged through the sea, and Rachel almost fell off her dolphin's back in surprise. It was going so fast – she felt as if she were flying!

Great cheers of excitement went up as the spectators on the beach spotted the dolphins, and the three fairies hunched low by the animals' fins, not wanting to be seen. The dolphins were closing in on the water-skiing goblin. Then, suddenly, all three of them leaped out of the water at once, making the goblin jump in surprise.

The startled goblin lost his balance and tumbled into the sea...dropping the piece of Golden Conch Shell as he fell!

"Oh no!" he yelled in dismay, his arms flailing as he tried to catch it. Echo was too quick for him, though. With another deft leap into the air, she caught the piece of shell in her mouth and dived back into the water.

The other two dolphins that Kirsty and Rachel were riding on followed, and, once they were all a safe distance from the goblins, the girls slipped off their backs.

"Thank you," Kirsty said, patting her dolphin's silky body. "I enjoyed that so much."

Meanwhile, Ally was hugging Echo, delighted to have the piece of Golden Conch Shell. "Well done, Echo," she said happily. "And well done, Kirsty and Rachel! I'd better take Echo and this piece of shell back to the Fairyland Royal Aquarium now, but I'm sure we'll meet again. I'll send you two back to your world – thanks for everything!"

Kirsty and Rachel hugged the smiling fairy, and Echo, too. They would never forget their wonderful dolphin adventure!

Then Ally waved her wand and a stream of silver sparkles whirled around them all, so that everything seemed to blur before their eyes. When the sparkly whirlwind died down again, the girls were back on the beach at Lea-on-Sea, behind the very same cluster of rocks where they'd started their fairy adventure.

"We've only been gone a minute," Kirsty said as she looked up to check the time on the clock tower. Then she smiled at Rachel. "That was the most exciting minute of my life, I think."

Rachel was smiling too, as she gazed out at the waves tumbling onto the shore. "I can't wait for our next ocean adventure," she said. "I think we're in for a very magical holiday!"

Now Kirsty and Rachel must help...

Amelie the Seal Fairy

Read on for a sneak peek...

"Look at the lighthouse, Rachel!" Kirsty Tate exclaimed to her best friend, Rachel Walker. "Isn't it beautiful?"

Rachel shaded her eyes from the sun and gazed at the lighthouse. The tall, newly-painted red and white building stood proudly among the rocks at the harbour entrance. "It's lovely," Rachel agreed admiringly. "It looks so much better than it did before."

"Everyone in town helped raise the money to renovate the lighthouse and turn it into an artists' studio," Kirsty's gran explained. Kirsty and Rachel were spending the spring holiday with her in the coastal resort of Leamouth. "There's been a lot of work going on since the last time you were here."

Rachel and Kirsty glanced at each other and smiled. On their previous visit to Leamouth, they'd met Shannon the Ocean Fairy and the girls had helped her to recover the three precious Enchanted Pearls that had been stolen by Jack Frost and his naughty goblin servants.

Now Rachel and Kirsty were in the middle of another thrilling fairy adventure. At the start of their holiday, King Oberon and Queen Titania had invited the girls to come to the Fairyland Ocean Gala which was held on the beach outside the Royal Aquarium.

There, Rachel and Kirsty had seen Shannon again, as well as her friends, the seven Ocean Fairies - Ally the Dolphin Fairy, Amelie the Seal Fairy, Pia the Penguin Fairy, Tess the Sea Turtle Fairy, Stephanie the Starfish Fairy, Whitney the Whale Fairy and Courtney the Clownfish Fairy.

The highlight of the Ocean Gala was the moment when Shannon played the Magical Golden Conch Shell, which would bring peace and order to the oceans of Fairyland and the human world for the coming year.

But just as she was about to do so, wicked Jack Frost had appeared and ordered his goblins to grab the Golden Conch Shell. As the goblins argued and fought with each other, the shell had fallen to the ground and shattered into seven shining pieces.

Immediately, a bolt of icy magic from Jack Frost's wand had sent the pieces whirling away into the human world, leaving Rachel, Kirsty and the fairies horrified. They knew that without the Golden Conch Shell, there would be chaos in the oceans.

"Last time we were in Leamouth, Jack Frost was up to his old tricks," Kirsty whispered to Rachel, as her gran walked off along the path to the lighthouse. "And now we're back again, so is *he*! We *must* find all the pieces of the Conch Shell, Rachel, so that it can be put back together again."

"Don't forget that the Magical Ocean Creatures will be guarding those missing pieces," Rachel reminded her.

Luckily, Queen Titania had acted quickly after mean Jack Frost and his goblins had vanished. Inside the Royal Aquarium, she'd shown the girls the seven Magical Ocean Creatures who belonged to the Ocean Fairies – a dolphin, a seal, a penguin, a turtle, a starfish, a whale and a clownfish, all of them glittering faintly with golden fairy magic. Then, with a wave of the queen's wand, the creatures had vanished. Queen Titania's spell had sent them into the human world to seek out and guard the seven missing fragments of shell until Kirsty, Rachel and the Ocean Fairies could find them and bring them back to Fairyland...

Read *Amelie the Seal Fairy* **to find out what adventures are in store for Kirsty and Rachel!**

Meet the Friendship Fairies

When Jack Frost steals the Friendship Fairies' magical objects, BFFs everywhere are in trouble! Can Rachel and Kirsty help save the magic of friendship?

www.rainbowmagicbooks.co.uk

Calling all parents, carers and teachers!
The Rainbow Magic fairies are here to help your child enter the magical world of reading. Whatever reading stage they are at, there's a Rainbow Magic book for everyone! Here is Lydia the Reading Fairy's guide to supporting your child's journey at all levels.

1

Starting Out

Our Rainbow Magic Beginner Readers are perfect for first-time readers who are just beginning to develop reading skills and confidence. Approved by teachers, they contain a full range of educational levelling, as well as lively full-colour illustrations.

2

Developing Readers

Rainbow Magic Early Readers contain longer stories and wider vocabulary for building stamina and growing confidence. These are adaptations of our most popular Rainbow Magic stories, specially developed for younger readers in conjunction with an Early Years reading consultant, with full-colour illustrations.

3

Going Solo

The Rainbow Magic chapter books – a mixture of series and one-off specials – contain accessible writing to encourage your child to venture into reading independently. These highly collectible and much-loved magical stories inspire a love of reading to last a lifetime.

www.rainbowmagicbooks.co.uk

"Rainbow Magic got my daughter reading chapter books. Great sparkly covers, cute fairies and traditional stories full of magic that she found impossible to put down" – Mother of Edie (6 years)

"Florence LOVES the Rainbow Magic books. She really enjoys reading now" – Mother of Florence (6 years)

The Rainbow Magic Reading Challenge

Well done, fairy friend – you have completed the book!
This book was worth 5 points.

See how far you have climbed on the
Reading Rainbow opposite.

The more books you read, the more points you will get,
and the closer you will be to becoming a Fairy Princess!

How to get your Reading Rainbow

1. Cut out the coin below
2. Go to the Rainbow Magic website
3. Download and print out your poster
4. Add your coin and climb up the Reading Rainbow!

There's all this and lots more at
www.rainbowmagicbooks.co.uk

You'll find activities, competitions, stories, a special
newsletter and complete profiles of all the
Rainbow Magic fairies. Find a fairy with your name!